DISCARDED

It's Raining, It's Pouring

For Jack ...
whose name requires a giant.
A.S.

For Peter ... who is one.
L.E.W.

Text copyright © 2001 Brandywine Enterprises BC Ltd.
Illustration copyright © 2001 Leslie Elizabeth Watts

Canadian Cataloguing in Publication Data
Spalding, Andrea.
It's raining, it's pouring

ISBN 1-55143-186-6

I. Watts, Leslie Elizabeth, 1961 – II. Title.
PS8587.P213I87 2001   jC813'.54 C00-911357-6
PZ7.S7334It 2001

Library of Congress Catalog Card Number: 00-110528

Orca Book Publishers gratefully acknowledges the support of our publishing
programs provided by the following agencies: the Department of Canadian Heritage,
The Canada Council for the Arts, and the British Columbia Arts Council.

Design by Christine Toller
Printed and bound in Hong Kong

IN CANADA:
Orca Book Publishers
PO Box 5626, Station B
Victoria, BC Canada
V8R 6S4

IN THE UNITED STATES:
Orca Book Publishers
PO Box 468
Custer, WA USA
98240-0468

03 02 01 • 5 4 3 2 1

It's Raining, It's Pouring

written by Andrea Spalding
illustrated by Leslie Elizabeth Watts

ORCA BOOK PUBLISHERS

LITTLE GIRL KNELT ON A CHAIR and gazed through the window. The rain made everything blurry, and the thunder made her jump.

"I hate thunder," said Little Girl.

"It's only Old Man. He's snoring again," smiled her mother. And she began to sing.

"It's raining, it's pouring,
The Old Man is snoring,
He went to bed with a cold in his head,
And he didn't get up in the morning.
Rain, rain, go away,
Little Girl wants to play."

"Why is Old Man in bed with a cold in his head?" asked Little Girl.

Her mother shrugged.

"All right," said Little Girl. "I'll go and find out."

She pulled on her rubber boots and tugged on her yellow raincoat. She plonked her fire fighter's helmet firmly on her head and stomped down into the basement to find the ladder.

The ladder was heavy. She heaved it out of the corner.
The ladder was wobbly. She wedged it against the wall.
The ladder was very laddery.
Little Girl climbed through the basement ceiling and into the middle of the kitchen.
"Be back before supper," waved her mother.

She climbed through the kitchen ceiling and entered the bedroom.

"Hold on tight," warned her father.

The ladder stretched through the bedroom, poked through the attic skylight and laddered its way up to the nearest thundercloud.

Little Girl climbed skyward.

The wind whistled and the rain ran off her helmet. The thunder muttered and the ladder shivered. She clung with her fingers and clutched with her arms and gripped with her teeth and braced with her feet.

Little Girl climbed right to the top and stepped out onto a soggy greyness.

"Where are you, Old Man?" she called.

The thunder rumbled.

"All right," said Little Girl. "I'll come and find you."

THIS WAY TO THE OLD MAN pointed a dripping sign.

"Good job I've got boots," she said as she squelched through the sogginess.

Little Girl stopped and stared.

There was the largest bed she'd ever seen.

In it lay a moaning, groaning giant. He'd balanced an ice pack on his head and stuck a thermometer in his mouth.

Little Girl climbed onto the bed and poked him gently. "Why are you in bed?"

The giant opened one eye, then closed it quickly.

"My head hurts, my eyes won't stop watering, my throat tickles, and I've a terrible cold." He sneezed, and the thunder rumbled and the cloud shook in sympathy.

"My mom gives me hot honey and lemon to drink when I've a cold," said Little Girl.

The giant cried, "But I haven't got a mom." He howled and the lightning flashed and the hail rattled around them.

"Oh." Little Girl thought for a moment. "I'll be right back."

Little Girl stomped through the rain and hail, found the top of the ladder and climbed down into the kitchen.

"Mom," she said, "Old Man's got a bad cold. I need honey and lemon. Lots of it … a whole wheelbarrow full."

"All right," said her mother. She made a warm, comforting drink and poured it into the wheelbarrow. "Would Old Man like some gingerbread cookies?"

"Oh, yes." Little Girl smiled happily. "And a nice warm hot water bottle, please," and she ran off to find her backpack and some rope.

First she packed the hot water bottle, then several long, woolly scarves. Finally, she carefully tucked the gingerbread cookies in the folds, where they wouldn't break. Little Girl hoisted her pack on her back.

Next, Little Girl tied one end of the gigantic rope around the wheelbarrow, and the other end around her body. She looped the coils over her shoulder and headed up the ladder again. Steadily through the kitchen, calmly through the bedroom, carefully through the attic and courageously through the skylight and up towards the clouds.

"Don't shake the ladder, Old Man," she yelled. "I'm hauling a big load."

The wind whistled and the rain ran off her helmet, but she clung with her fingers, clutched with her arms, gripped with her teeth and braced with her feet, and she didn't drop the barrow.

Little Girl wheeled the barrow to the bed and heaved herself up on the quilt.

"Here," she said, and unpacked.

Old Man sat up and looked interested.

Little Girl swathed the scarves around his neck and tucked the hot water bottle by his feet. Then very, very, VERY carefully she leaned over the edge of the bed and hauled up the wheelbarrow.

"Aaaah," began the giant as his nose tickled.

"Don't you dare," said Little Girl. "I mustn't spill."

"Aaah … BROoooo!" The giant stopped his sneeze just in time. The bed trembled, but the drink stayed in the barrow.

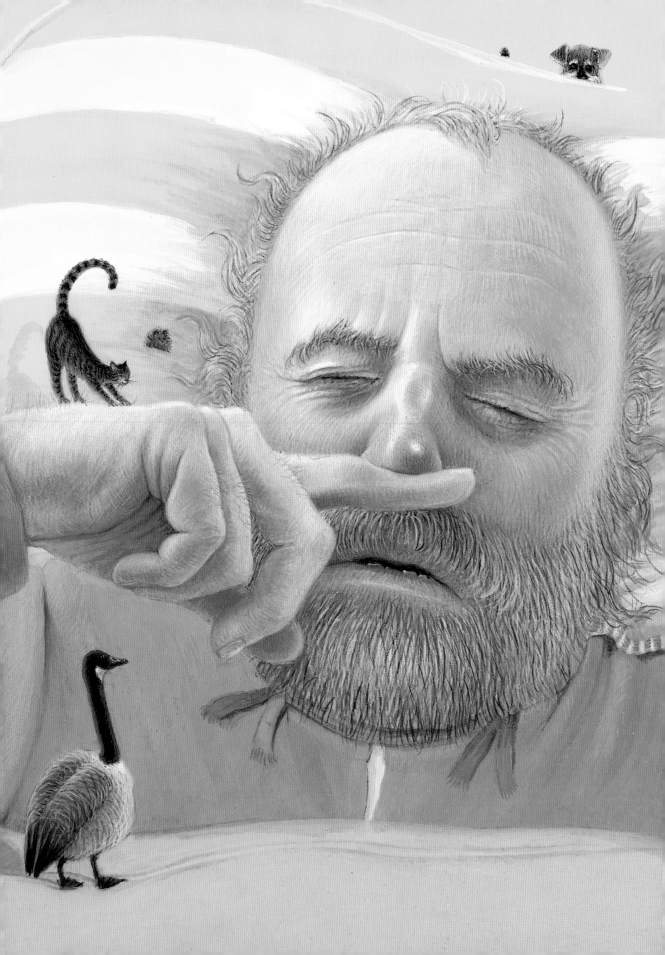

Old Man clasped his hands around the barrow. "This feels nice and warm," he said approvingly.

He took a long and noisy sip. "This tastes honey and lemoney."

He slurped noisily. "This stops my throat tickling and my nose prickling."

He swigged and he swilled and he guzzled and he gulped. Down to the very last drop.

Little Girl munched on a cookie and offered the other to Old Man.

"Ummm, I feel … BETTER," smiled Old Man, and he chomped the cookie with a giant-sized bite.

The sun came out.

"Quick," cried Old Man. "You'd better hurry back."

Little Girl threw the hot water bottle into the barrow and trundled towards the ladder. The cloud turned steamy and thin. The squelchiness turned to softness and the greyness turned to blue.

She leaped for the top of the ladder.

"Hold on," called Old Man, "and thank you."

And he shot a sunbeam through the gap in the cloud.

Little Girl caught the sunbeam and slid and slithered and swirled and slipped all the way down the ladder and into her house.

She pulled off her boots, took off her coat, hung up her fire fighter's helmet and put away her backpack. Carefully she unladdered the ladder and stowed it in the corner of the basement.

Finally, she wheeled the empty barrow back to her mother.

"There," she said, "that fixed him."

And she put on her runners …

... and went out to play.